D0832609

characters created by
lauren child
I WANT
to be much
more bigger
like you
PUFFIN

Charlie and Lola®

Text based on the script written by Carol Noble

Illustrations from the TV animation produced by Tiger Aspe

PUFFIN BOOKS
Published by the Penguin Group: London, New York, Australia,
Canada, India, Ireland, New Zealand and South Africa
Penguin Books Ltd, Registered Offices: 80 Strand, London WC2R 0RL, England

puffinbooks.com

This edition published in Great Britain in Puffin Books 2012
001 – 10 9 8 7 6 5 4 3 2 1

Charlie and Lola is produced by Tiger Aspect Productions

Manufactured in China
ISBN: 978-0-718-19524-3
This edition produced for the Book People Ltd,
Hall Wood Avenue, Haydock, St Helens, WA11 9UL

I have this little sister Lola.
She is small and very funny.
Lola says, "I'm not small, Charlie.
I am getting more **bigger**
and grown-up all of the time."

"And now that I am
much more bigger,
I can go on the
Super-Duper Loopy Loopy ride."

So I say,
"The Super-Duper
Loop the Looper is very, very SCARY.
Are you sure?"

"I am very sure, Charlie," says Lola.

So I measure Lola to see
if she really is **bigger**.

"Charlie, I must be more **taller** than that!
Are you **tricking** me?"

"No, Lola. That's exactly how **big** you are."

Then Lola says,
"But I absolutely MUST be
big enough to go on the
Super-Duper Loopy Loopy ride."

I say,
"There are still loads of
fun rides at the fair
for smaller people.

The **Chug-a-Bugs** ride
is **really** exciting."

And Lola says,
"I **don't** think so, Charlie."

Then Lola says,
“I have a GOOD plan.
I am going to think myself bigger.

Now I am thinking I am nearly
as big as a sunflower
touching the sun...

"And now I am thinking
I am as **big** as one of those

extremely

TALLEST

buildings."

I say,
"You can't MAKE yourself **bigger**, Lola.
It just happens."

Lola says, "It's not fair. Why am I always, always the small one?"

So I say, "There are great things about being small. Like...

"... you get **stories** read
to you every night...

and you get loads of **piggybacks**."

But Lola says,
"I still really, **really** would
like being the **biggest**."

When Marv comes over, he says,
"Are you ready for the
Super-Duper Loop the Looper?"

And Lola shouts,
"I am! I am! I am!"

Then Marv whispers,

"She's quite **small** for the ride,

isn't she, Charlie?"

And I say, "Yup."

At the fair, Marv says,
"The **Super-Duper Loop the Looper**
is going to be the best ride!"

"Yes. It will make our hair
stand on end," I say.

"And our tummies go all funny,"
says Marv.
"I can't wait! How about you, Lola?"

"Err... I can't wait either..."

When we get to the front of the line,
Marv says,
"Hold on to your tummy, Lola!"

But Lola says,
"Err... I think I might be slightly too small still.

Perhaps it would be
a little more fun if I went on
something for more slightly
smaller people – like the
Chug-a-Bugs!"

So we all go on the **Chug-a-Bugs** and Lola **laughs** and **laughs**.

She says, "You were right, Charlie! The **Chug-a-Bugs** IS the very best ride in the whole world and the universe."